21st Century
Basic Skills
Library

BABY ZOO ANIMALS
POLAR BEARS

by Josh Gregory

Cherry Lake Publishing • Ann Arbor, Michigan

3

Published in the United States of America
by Cherry Lake Publishing
Ann Arbor, Michigan
www.cherrylakepublishing.com

Content Adviser: Dr. Stephen S. Ditchkoff, Professor of Wildlife Sciences, Auburn University, Auburn, Alabama

Photo Credits: Cover and page 1, ©Stayer/Shutterstock, Inc.; page 4, ©marchello_/Shutterstock, Inc.; pages 6, 10, and 20, ©Tomas Hajek/Dreamstime.com; page 8, ©Outdoorsman/Dreamstime.com; page 12, ©Helen E. Grose/Dreamstime.com; page 14, ©Olga Sapegina/Shutterstock, Inc.; page 16, ©Gea Strucks/Dreamstime.com; page 18, ©Christoph Hilger/Dreamstime.com

Library of Congress Cataloging-in-Publication Data
Gregory, Josh.
  Polar bears / by Josh Gregory.
      p. cm. — (21st century basic skills library) (Baby zoo animals)
  Includes bibliographical references and index.
  ISBN 978-1-61080-459-2 (lib. bdg.) — ISBN 978-1-61080-546-9 (e-book) — ISBN 978-1-61080-633-6 (pbk.)
  1. Polar bear—Infancy—Juvenile literature. 2. Zoo animals—Infancy—Juvenile literature. I. Title.
  SF408.6.P64G74 2013
  599.786092'9—dc23   2012001730

Cherry Lake Publishing would like to acknowledge
the work of The Partnership for 21st Century Skills.
Please visit www.21stcenturyskills.org for more information.

Printed in the United States of America
Corporate Graphics Inc.
July 2012
CLFA11

TABLE OF CONTENTS

Small, White, and Furry

Have you seen a **polar bear**?

These big, white bears live in the **Arctic**.

You can also see them at zoos. You might even see a baby polar bear!

Baby polar bears are called **cubs**.

Mother polar bears have one to four cubs at a time.

Newly born cubs are tiny. Their fur is very thin. They look almost hairless!

Wild polar bears live where the weather is very cold.

Polar bears have heavy fur to protect them from this weather.

Polar Bear Life

Polar bears at zoos spend most of their time resting or sleeping.

They also like to swim in pools of cold water.

Cubs drink milk from their mothers for about 2 years.

Adult polar bears mostly eat meat and fish.

Polar bear cubs usually stay close to their mothers.

Adult polar bears are quiet. Cubs like to make sounds.

They use many different sounds to **communicate** with their mothers.

Getting Bigger

Polar bear cubs grow very quickly.

They learn to walk when they are around 2 months old.

Their fur grows thicker.

Three-month-old cubs weigh about 30 pounds (13.6 kilograms). This is around the same size as a four-year-old child.

Cubs weigh three times that amount when they are 1 year old.

Polar bears become adults when they are between 4 and 6 years old. Then they **mate** to have cubs.

Then there are new babies at the zoo!

Find Out More

BOOK

Hatkoff, Juliana. *Knut: The Baby Polar Bear*. New York: Scholastic, 2008.

WEB SITE

San Diego Zoo—Animal Bytes: Polar Bear
www.sandiegozoo.org/animalbytes/t-polar_bear.html
Read facts and check out pictures of polar bears.

Glossary

Arctic (ARK-tik) the area around the North Pole

communicate (kuh-MYOO-ni-kate) share information, ideas, or feelings

cubs (KUBZ) babies of certain animals, such as polar bears

mate (MATE) join together to produce babies

polar bear (POH-lur BAYR) large, white bear that lives in the Arctic

Home and School Connection

Use this list of words from the book to help your child become a better reader. Word games and writing activities can help beginning readers reinforce literacy skills.

a	born	hairless	mother	sounds	usually
about	called	have	mothers	spend	very
adult	can	heavy	new	stay	walk
adults	child	in	newly	swim	water
almost	close	is	of	that	weather
also	cold	kilograms	old	the	weigh
amount	communicate	learn	one	their	when
and	cubs	life	or	them	where
Arctic	different	like	polar	then	white
are	drink	live	pools	there	wild
around	eat	look	pounds	these	with
as	even	make	protect	they	year
at	fish	many	quickly	thicker	years
babies	for	mate	quiet	thin	you
baby	four	meat	resting	this	zoo
bear	from	might	same	three	zoos
bears	fur	milk	see	time	
become	furry	month	seen	times	
between	getting	months	size	tiny	
big	grow	most	sleeping	to	
bigger	grows	mostly	smaller	use	

Fast Facts

Habitat: Arctic, tundra, and forests

Range: Far northern areas of Alaska, Canada, Greenland, Russia, and Norway

Average Length: 6.6 to 10 feet (2 to 3 meters)

Average Weight: Males usually weigh between 660 and 1,760 pounds (300 and 800 kilograms). Females weigh between 330 and 660 pounds (150 and 300 kg).

Life Span: Males live about 15 to 18 years in the wild. Females live into their mid 20s. Captive polar bears live longer than wild ones.

Index

About the Author

Josh Gregory writes and edits books for children. He lives in Chicago, Illinois.